No More Biscuits!

A Florence and Arnold Story

For Emily and her friends who used to play at dressing up – PL
For Faye and Phoebe – BG

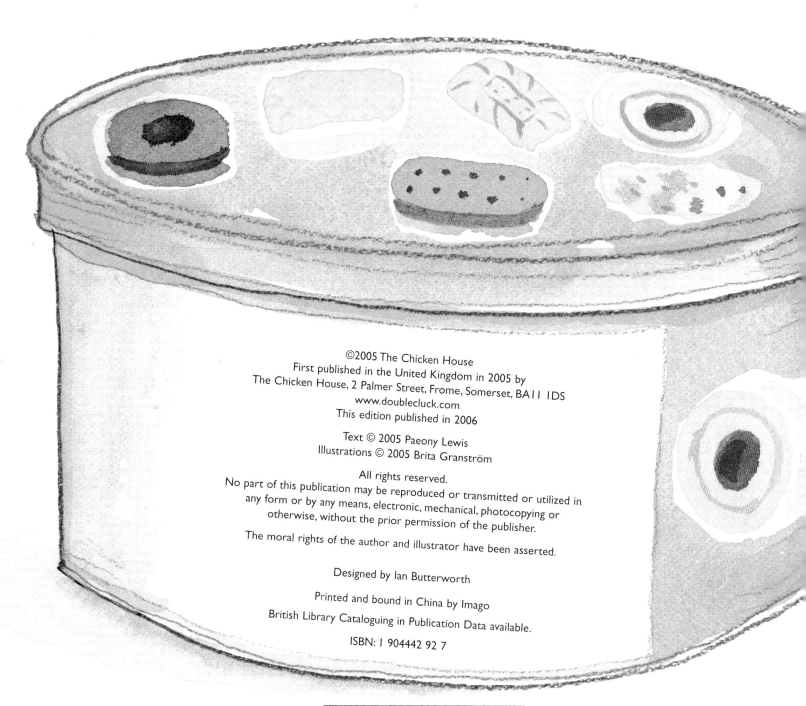

©2005 The Chicken House
First published in the United Kingdom in 2005 by
The Chicken House, 2 Palmer Street, Frome, Somerset, BA11 1DS
www.doublecluck.com
This edition published in 2006

Text © 2005 Paeony Lewis
Illustrations © 2005 Brita Granström

Designed by Ian Butterworth

Printed and bound in China by Imago
British Library Cataloguing in Publication Data available.

ISBN: 1 904442 92 7

No More Biscuits!

A Florence and Arnold Story
by Paeony Lewis Illustrated by Brita Granström

2 Palmer Street, Frome, Somerset BA11 1DS

I'm Florence and this is Arnold. He is helping me to decide which is my favourite biscuit.

Mum stares at the empty biscuit tin.

We didn't mean to eat all the biscuits.
It just happened. I say sorry.

Mum says I'm a biscuit monster
and no more biscuits for a week.

I tell her that Arnold ate some too.
And there's another packet in the cupboard.

She still says,

NO more biscuits.

No biscuits for a week. That's for ever.
We pretend we're secret agents,
and think up plans
to get biscuits.

But Arnold says he's hungry and the plans won't work. He changes his mind when he hears my new idea. I find what we need in the dressing-up box.

All we want is a biscuit — just one.

I tell Mum I'm Florence the tooth fairy. I've had a busy night collecting teeth and my fairy monkey and me need a biscuit before we can fly home.

Mum shakes her head. She says she can't give biscuits to tooth fairies. They're bad for teeth. Instead she gives me an apple. Plus another for my fairy monkey.

It's **not** fair!

All we want is a **biscuit** – just **one**.

This time we creep up behind Mum at the washing machine. I tell her I'm Florence the wickedest witch in the world. If she doesn't give us a biscuit then my magic monkey will turn her into a frog!

Mum laughs. She says she'd like to be a frog because frogs don't have to wash smelly clothes. So, *no* biscuits.

It's not fair. All we want is a biscuit
– just one.

The next biscuit plan is Arnold's idea. It's a good one.

I cycle from the back garden to the front door. Carefully, I lay Arnold and my bike on the path. Red paint shines on his fur.

I tell Arnold to look sad as I knock on the door.

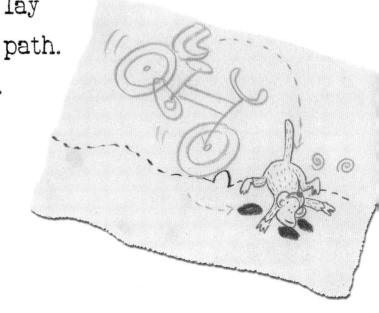

Mum opens our door and says hello.

I tell her I'm Florence the nurse and
I've found a monkey who's fallen off his bike.
He's hurt and needs an emergency biscuit.

emergency biscuit Ambulance

Mum groans. She says, *no* biscuits.
Injured monkeys need medicine and bandages.

It's not **fair.**

All we want is a biscuit – just one.

Arnold can't think of another biscuit plan. He just sits there in his bandages, looking hungry.

I hunt deep inside my dressing-up
box and pull out a silver crown.
Maybe I could be a queen and
command Mum to give us
biscuits. But Arnold thinks not.
Mum never does what she's told.

All we want
is a **biscuit**
– just one.

What can we do?
        Suddenly, I grab Arnold and give him
                a hug. I've thought of the best biscuit
                        plan in the world.

We find Mum picking green beans in the garden. I say hello, I'm Florence the famous chef. My monkey assistant knows how to cook something nicer than beans. Yummy biscuits! Mum frowns. She says no biscuits. NO. NO.

NO!

Arnold feels like crying.
All we want is a biscuit — just one.

I think Mum feels bad for being
so mean to Arnold.

She says we can COOK . . .

Magic Monkey Bananas!

We're top chefs.

Mum's in charge of the hot water.

Arnold and me stir the chocolate

Arnold
pours
on
too
many
sprinkles.

The bananas go in the
freezer and we clear up.
Mum tells me not to lick
chocolate off Arnold's fur.

At teatime we don't ask for boring biscuits.
All we want are Magic Monkey Bananas.
Just one for me.
Just one for Arnold.

And tWO for . . .

...my lovely mum!

Magic Monkey Bananas

Magic Monkey

Bananas ---->

INGREDIENTS FOR FOUR
2 bananas
100g of chocolate
2 tablespoons of
multi-coloured sprinkles

You'll also need:
One grown-up to help you
do the difficult bits!
4 lolly sticks (or similar)
1 sheet of baking parchment
(greaseproof paper)

TO MAKE FOUR MAGIC MONKEY BANANAS:

FIRST get a grown-up to melt all the
chocolate in a bowl over hot water or
use the microwave.

NOW peel two firm bananas and
cut each one in half so you have
four halves.

THEN push lolly sticks in the cut
end of each halved banana.

NEXT hold the lolly stick and dip
the halved banana in the melted
chocolate – use a spoon to help!
Things might get a bit messy,
but who cares? It's chocolate!

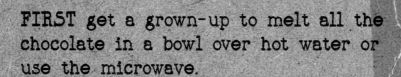

SHAKE sprinkles over the gooey chocolate-covered banana.

PLACE the coated banana on a sheet of baking parchment (on a plastic plate) and repeat until they're all done.

PUT the plate of banana lollies in the freezer for at least one hour. That's for ever!

WHILE you are waiting, do the cleaning up. Don't forget to lick the chocolate off the bowl and spoon!

FINALLY remove the lollies from the freezer and . . .

...eat your Magic Monkey Banana! **YUM!**

Magic Monkey Bananas are great for sharing with your favourite people.

And **monkeys** too!

For most chocolate

Just lick around.